Richard Scarry's
Busy Day Storybooks

Miss Honey's
Busy Day

J.B. COMMUNICATIONS INC.

The sun is up!
Miss Honey and Bruno wake from their sleep.

"Good morning, Bruno," says Miss Honey.
"Good morning, Miss Honey!" says Bruno, yawning.
"Did you sleep well?"

4

While Miss Honey
washes her face
and brushes her teeth
in the bathroom,
Bruno gets dressed.

Don't forget to wash,
too, Bruno!

Miss Honey and Bruno go to the kitchen.
Bruno sits down at the table.

"What would you like
for breakfast today, Bruno?"
Miss Honey asks.
"Chocolate ice cream, please!"
replies Bruno.

"But, Bruno," says Miss Honey, "you had chocolate ice cream for breakfast yesterday."

"Hmmm," thinks Bruno, "then today I'll have pistachio, OK?"

Bruno drives Miss Honey to school
in his ice cream truck.

At the school door,
she waves goodbye to him.
Soon schoolchildren arrive.

"Good morning, pupils!" Miss Honey says.
"Good morning, Miss Honey!" reply the children.

9

The children take their seats in the classroom,
and Miss Honey checks the attendance list.

"Hilda? Huckle? Lowly?... Vanderbuilt?" she asks.
"Where is Vanderbuilt?"

Aa Bb Cc Dd Ee Ff Gg Hh Ii Jj Kk Ll Mm Nn

Suddenly Vanderbuilt appears in the door.
"Excuse me for being late, Miss Honey," Vanderbuilt says,
"Uncle Gronkle's car wouldn't start this morning!"

First, the class practices spelling.
"Who knows how to spell APPLE?"
asks Miss Honey.

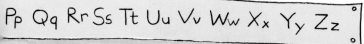

Lowly spells, "A-P-P-L-E, apple!"
Good for you, Lowly!

Next, the class works with numbers.
Miss Honey asks Vanderbuilt to do
an addition.
Miss Honey is patient and helps
Vanderbuilt find the answer.

The class bell rings.
It's time for gym!

The pupils leave the classroom
to change into their sports uniforms
in the locker room.

The class plays a
game of basketball
with Mr. Tough.
It's lots of fun!

Flossy Bunny shoots
the ball into the net.

Good shot, Flossy!

14

After gym, it's time for lunch.
The children join Miss Honey
in the school cafeteria.
There are many different
things to choose from.

"Try to choose
items from
more than one
food group,"
Miss Honey
says. "That's
the way to keep
healthy!"

Then it's time for recess.
While everyone plays outside
in the school playground,
Miss Honey gives Bruno
a telephone call.

"What did you have
for lunch today, Bruno?"
Miss Honey asks.
"Ice cream!" replies Bruno.

"Bruno, you have to eat
something other than
just ice cream!" says
Miss Honey.
"Okay, Miss Honey, I
promise. Tomorrow I will
eat something different."

This afternoon, Miss Honey has a special treat for her class: a field trip to the Busytown Fire Station!

The class rides to the firehouse in the school bus.

Smokey greets them at the door.

"Wow!" says Huckle. "This is neat!"

The children learn all about the fire truck and the firefighters' duties, and Snozzle brings everyone refreshments.

As a surprise, the firefighters drive the class back to school in the fire engine.

Aren't they lucky! I think Miss Honey enjoys the return ride, too.

Back in the classroom, Miss Honey asks the pupils to make a drawing of the fire station to bring in to school tomorrow.

The school bell rings, and Miss Honey's class heads home.
What a busy day it has been! Look! Here comes Bruno!
He has brought Miss Honey a rose.

"May I invite you
out to dinner
tonight, Miss
Honey?" he asks.
"Why, I'd be
delighted. Thank
you!" says Miss
Honey. "Where
shall we go?"

Why, of course, to Bruno's favorite:
the ice cream parlor!